The Real Boy Wizard

SULLY PRIMARY SCHOOL
Burnham Avenue
Sully
Vale of Glamorgan
CF64 5SU
Tel: 029 20 530377

The Real Boy Wizard

E. R. Reilly

© E.R. Reilly, 2011

Published by   Santiago Press
                PO Box 8808
                Birmingham
                B30 2LR

Email for orders and enquiries:
santiago@reilly19.freesereve.co.uk

Illustrations © Jonathan Russell, 2011

ISBN: 978-0-9562568-4-3

Prepared by:

York Publishing Services Ltd
64 Hallfield Road
Layerthorpe
York YO31 7ZQ
Tel: 01904 431213

Website: www.yps-publishing.co.uk

Printed and bound in India by Authentic Media
A division of OM Books Foundation, Secunderabad 500 067, India
E-mail: printing@ombooks.org

CONTENTS

Chapter 1 – Finding my powers

This book is not like any other book that you will ever read. I am a real boy wizard and this is my story. Do not expect broomsticks and potions. This is a not a make believe story. This is a real story. I cannot reveal my identity, but I may be somebody you know. I may be a boy in your school or in your street. I may even be related to you. I don't know if I am the only real boy wizard. I hope that there is another boy wizard. I hope that there is another boy wizard out there somewhere. If there is a girl who has the same powers I hope that my story lets him or her know that they're not alone. I may be the only real boy wizard in the whole world. That's probably the hardest thing. I can't talk to anybody about my powers. I don't know why I've got them and I don't know what I'm supposed to do with them. I know that I can't talk to anybody about them and it's a lonely life.

Most of the time I'm just like any normal boy. I live with my mum and dad and I don't have any brothers or sisters. I go to a normal school. I like my teacher. I've got some nice friends (and one really bad enemy), but of course none of them know that I'm a real boy wizard. It's not the kind of thing that you could tell somebody. I know how I would feel if somebody were to tell me that they were a real wizard. I would think that they were mad – if I didn't know that such a thing really existed. I knew from the moment that I realized I was a real boy wizard I could never tell anybody about my special powers.

I know that anybody who thinks about wizards tends to think about Merlin or Harry Potter. The truth about being a real boy wizard is very different to that. To begin with:

I can't control my powers. I don't know when my powers are going to come and I don't know how they are going to affect me. Each time my powers come on, I start out upon a new adventure. I have powers that I can't explain. I don't know why I've been given powers. I don't know what I'm supposed to do with them. All I know is that I get transformed into different people at different times in history and I have powers that help me on my adventures. I sometimes think that I'm just supposed to learn as much as I can about the places my adventures take me to. I don't know what I'm supposed to learn or why I'm supposed to learn it. It's not easy being the only real boy wizard. I don't know why I have these powers. I don't know what I'm supposed to do with them and worst of all I can't tell anybody about them.

The first time that I found out about my special powers I was on holiday by the seaside and I suddenly found myself in my first adventure with pirates and smugglers. I'm going to tell you about my adventures. Maybe this story will be read by another boy or girl who has the same powers as me. If you are a boy or a girl wizard and you have the same powers as me, at least you will know from my story that you are not the only one with these powers.

On the day of my first adventure my parents left me sitting on a blanket. We were at the seaside and my parents went into the sea for a swim. As I waved to them I felt myself drifting away into another time and into another place. I could feel that I was leaving my own body behind and becoming somebody very different. I was on hot sands on a hot day. There was somebody shouting to me to get a move on, and somebody else shouting: "Over here. I've found one of them."

I was wearing baggy trousers. I had a red and white bandanna and I was carrying a dagger. The man running after me was shouting: "I can see one of the pirates, follow me men."

All the men chasing me were British sailors. Their uniforms were from a long time ago. I knew I was

in England, but I don't know how I knew. I wasn't a small child anymore. I was a man with huge muscles. I ran towards some rocks and my friend pulled me up. We ran up onto the top of a hill where some other friends were waiting in a coach. We jumped into the coach and the horses reared up and roared off at racing speed. They threw us from side to side as they raced around the country lanes. We were all laughing and cheering. We had beaten the British navy once again!

My wizard powers had turned me into a pirate. Somehow I knew how to act. I knew what to do and how to do it, but I don't know how I knew. We pulled up at an old coaching Inn. The walls were black and white on the outside but just black on the inside. We left the evening sunshine outside. Inside it was black. It was very black and smoky. Every single man in there had a pipe in one hand and some grog or rum in the other. There was a small man behind the bar. He was bald on the top of his head but he had long straggly hair coming down to his shoulders. He had on an old baggy white shirt that looked more black than white. His skin was dark like tobacco and his teeth were as black as sin. He had a hunched back and a mean look. He poured rum into a row of glasses and pushed them towards us.

Billy the Blackheart raised a glass and said, "To the finest pirates on the seven seas."

Everyone raised their glasses and said, "To the finest pirates on the seven seas."

A jolly old man slapped me on the arm and told me to get myself over in the corner. I went and sat down in the corner and he said, "roll up your sleeve and I'll do that tattoo I promised you."

He got out some very sharp tools and some very black ink. I drank my rum and kept my face straight. I had to: I was a pirate.

Billy the Blackheart spoke again. "We have no time to waste lads. We know that the navy is looking for us. So fill your bellies full of rum. We're heading down to the docks. We'll gather some mutineers and sail off before first light. Joyless Jack is going to tell you where."

Everybody knocked their tankards on the tables and Joyless Jack got up to speak.

"There's a ship sailing into Plymouth with a huge bounty on board. It has a treasure chest that's going to make everyone who has a part of it rich.

We have a pirate on board the ship who is passing himself off as a common trader. He'll be keeping the last watch and he won't raise the alarm. It will be the easiest plundering that we'll ever do. There'll be so much treasure and pieces of eight, and so much grog that we might get bad backs just trying to carry it all!"

All the pirates cheered and laughed and Joyless Jack said, "Are you with us?"

All of the pirates shouted "Yes", and set about finishing their rum and grog. The pirate doing my tattoo started drinking and dancing. He left me with half a Jolly Roger on my arm.

Coaches took us down to the docks where we hid in dark corners keeping a look out for mutineers. There were always mutineers, whenever a ship came in there were always those who jumped off and set about looking for a better voyage. We asked them if they wanted to sail under the Jolly Roger and if they said yes, and they usually did, then we took them on board with us. Mutineers were good to have on board. They knew how to sail. You could say, "Hoist the main brace," to them; and they would know what to do.

We hid in the dark alleyways between the tall buildings on the docks and soon enough some mutineers came running our way. They were being pursued by sailors. The sailors wanted to haul them back to their ship and make them do all of the hard work on the ship. It's hard work being a press ganger on a ship. Usually press gangers are men who get drunk. Sailors attack them and they wake up several miles out at sea and find that they have to work hard from morning until night so that they can get some food. That's why they try to escape as soon as they reach the dock, and that's why they're happy to join up with us and became pirates. When the mutineers said that they wanted to escape, we came out of the darkness and faced up to the sailors. Billy Blackheart and Joyless Jack were as fierce looking as any pirate that you have ever seen. With the rest of us standing behind them, we looked invincible. The sailors took one look at us, turned around and ran back towards their ship.

We moved along the docks a little in the dead of the night and headed out to our ship. Billy the Blackheart gave the orders and we sailed out to sea. There were chores to do, watches to keep and orders to be obeyed, but there was also a lot of rum to drink. We had three days of fair weather sailing ahead of us. We had biscuits to eat. You just knock the maggots off and dip them into the water to soften them up. When they're nice and soft you eat them, chew on a lime and wash it all down with rum.

In the evening we have music on squeeze boxes and fiddles, and we sing songs and dance. Sometimes we'll even have a ghost story or two. I like being a boy wizard if it sends me on adventures like this. Somehow I have the special power of knowing how to do stuff, but I don't know how to conjure up magic or use potions like you read about in books. Being a real boy wizard is so different to anything that you might have imagined.

I knew enough to keep on the right side of Billy Blackheart. It's a mistake to upset him in anyway. If you upset him a tiny little bit you get clasped in leg irons. If you upset him quite a bit you get clasped in body irons. If you upset him a lot you get the cat o' nine tails and if you really upset him you get to walk the plank. That's a one way track to a watery grave with Davey Jones' locker.

That's where pirates go when they die.

After three days sailing we came to the ship that we were set to plunder. We sent the signal to our man who had sneaked on board and passed himself off as a crew member on the ship. He had arranged to be on watch so that no alarm would be raised. It was a foggy night on a grey sea, so we managed to sail almost upon them. They were all asleep. This was going to be the easiest pirate attack in the history of the high seas. We came alongside, so close that we were only a sling shot away. Then we saw a sight that we thought we would never see. A plank was raised from the ship and a man was pushed onto it at sword point. It was our man. He had his mouth gagged and his hands were tied. They had made him walk the plank. Suddenly, we saw a sailor swinging through the air behind him and he kicked him to his watery grave. We had been tricked: They were waiting for us.

The air was filled with smoke and the sound of huge bangs filled the air. Cannon balls were shot from their ship to ours and their sailors swung across to our ship on long ropes. They landed with swords in the hands and pistols by their sides.

There was a terrific fight and it was dirty. There was punching and biting and kicking. Pistol shots were fired and sword fights were going on all around. Some of our pirates lowered a rowing boat and were making a

20

getaway. I ran to the edge of the boat and jumped over the side and into the water. I started to splash around frantically trying to get to the boat. The waves were throwing me backwards and were making it hard for me to get to the boat. I was getting deeper into the water.

Then I heard my name being called out. I recognized the sound of the voice but I couldn't make any sense of it. I looked all around but I couldn't see where the voice was coming from. Then suddenly, my mum was standing over me and I was lying in my bed. Mum was calling my name and telling me to get up. "Oh dear", she said, "never mind, you go and have a shower and I'll see to this."

I was in a daze. I had had my first real adventure as a real boy wizard and I had survived. But I didn't know why I had the powers and I didn't know how I could control them. I had been a pirate. I knew how to be a pirate. I could travel in time. I was more than an ordinary boy. I had special powers.

When I got to school Mrs Smith greeted me just the same way as she did every morning. She gave me a big smile and put her arms around me. You get lovely hugs from Mrs Smith. She's ever so kind. You have to be really naughty to be told off by Mrs Smith. If you fall over she cleans you up and puts a plaster on your knee. She clearly had no idea that I had discovered my new powers, that I could travel in time and that I had become a pirate. I wanted to tell her, but how do you tell someone that you are a real boy wizard? I wanted to tell everyone, but I knew that I couldn't tell anyone. They would think that I was mad.

Every day we have something called show, tell or talkabout. I put my hand up to talkabout pirates. I told the class about pirates. I told them how pirates wore baggy shorts and baggy shirts, how they had black tattoos, and how they drank grog or rum and ate biscuits (but that they knocked off the maggots first). I told them that pirates waited by the docks to recruit mutineers because they knew how to sail. I told them that pirates all smoke pipes, and dance to music played on squeeze boxes and fiddles.

Mrs Smith said that it was just about the best talkabout that she had ever heard. She said that anybody would think that I was a pirate because I know so much about them. She put a marble in the jar. That's what Mrs Smith does if somebody does some really good work. When the jar is full the whole class gets a treat. The next time the jar is full, we are going to visit the history museum to see the dinosaur skeleton and the fossils.

I like Mrs Smith: she always does nice things for us and we get nice treats. Best of all she gives us her special hugs and she loves us up.

Chapter 2 – Billy Big Ears

I hate Billy Big Ears. You would hate him too if he was in your class. This will give you an idea of what he's like. One day when we were doing a Maths test, Billy got out of his chair without anybody knowing. He crawled in between the tables and under Mrs Smith's table, took her sandwiches out of her bag and ate them. And Mrs Smith didn't even tell him off. She told him that he should have told her if he was hungry. That is so typical of Mrs Smith. She never tells anyone off. I wish she would tell Billy off. I hate him. I hate him. I hate him. I hate him. I hate him.

Last summer he brought matches into school and set fire to some grass and twigs on the school playing field. He's mean to everybody. He breaks everybody's toys and he's a bully. I hate him. I hate him. I hate him. I hate him. You have to hide from him when you have your snack at playtime because he makes you give him some all of the time. I refused to give him some crisps one time and he punched me in the stomach and pinched the bag out of my hand. He started to push me around in the playground after my "talkabout".

I wish I could use my wizard powers when I want to. I would use them on Billy Big Ears. I would turn myself into a pirate and I would bash him up. I would squeeze him tight in a bear hug and I would throw him to the ground. Then I would pick him up by his ears and swing him around.

Then I would throw him up against the wall and then I would stamp on his foot. Then I would pull him by his hair. I know what I would do then. I would take him out on a voyage with the pirates. I would tell Billy the Blackheart and Joyless Jack that he was stealing off other pirates – eating their biscuits and stealing their grog or their rum. That would be brilliant, we would put him in leg irons or body irons and we would give him the cat o' nine tails.

Then when he screamed for mercy we would say, "You never showed any mercy when you were stealing biscuits off good honest pirates did you?"

Then Billy the Blackheart would tell me that I could decide if he should be given mercy or whether he should be made to walk the plank. I would make him beg for mercy and when he had begged me over and over again I would say, "Sorry, no mercy". Then I would say at first light you must walk the plank. And at first light we'd lift him up onto the plank. And I would poke him with my sword to make him walk. I would keep poking him until he fell off into the sea, and with his hands bound tightly behind his back he would sink to a watery grave.

If I could summon up my wizard powers – that's what I would do.

Or maybe I wouldn't – I don't know. Maybe I'm supposed to learn what I'm supposed to do before I can choose when to use my powers. I'm confused. I don't think I would do all of those things to Billy even if I could. I wish I was stronger though so that he would know that I could bash him up if I wanted to.

Chapter 3 – Dinosaurs

Every time somebody does some good work in our class Mrs Smith puts a marble in a jar. When the jar is full we are all going to the dinosaur museum as a treat. We've got a nice class and Mrs Smith is really nice, so we get lots of marbles in the jar. It shouldn't be too long before we get to go to the museum, that's if Billy Big Ears doesn't spoil it; somehow he manages to spoil nearly everything in our class. We went to visit Cadbury World last year. Billy managed to spoil that. We were half way around the tour of Cadbury World and Billy started stealing chocolates and stuffing them in his pockets. There was no need for him to steal any chocolates, you get loads of free chocolates when you go to Cadbury World anyway. When the woman who was showing us around saw him, she told him to put them back, but instead of putting them back he ran off. He climbed out of a window and got stuck on a roof. They had to send for the fire brigade to come and get him down. This meant that we had to wait around for ages and by the time we were ready to finish the tour it was getting really late.

So we were rushed around the tour really quickly and when we got out it was so late the shop was shut. This meant we couldn't buy presents for our families and it was all because of Billy Big Ears. I hate him, I hate him, I hate him, I hate him, I hate him.

Every time I found myself looking forward to the museum visit I kept wondering how Billy was going to ruin it. I bet he will find a way to ruin it. He ruins everything. I hate him.

I try not to think about Billy too much. It just makes me angry. Although, I do like thinking of the ways that I would like to bash him up. When my mum reads to me at bedtime, she asks me about my day. I always tell her about how nice Mrs Smith is, and I tell her about my friends. I don't tell her much about Billy though. I don't want her to be upset. I don't want her to think that I'm weak either. I suppose that I really want her to think that I can look after myself. I wish I could talk to her more really. I would love to tell her that I'm a real boy wizard but of course I can't. I really can't tell anybody. Well, at least I can't tell anybody until I understand it better myself. Maybe I'm not supposed to tell anybody until I do fully understand it. And maybe I'm still not supposed to tell anybody. I'm just confused. If only I could meet just one other real boy wizard who could tell me everything that I need to know. It's the not knowing that's driving me mad. I don't know why I have wizard powers – I don't know how to control the powers. I don't know why I've been given these powers. There are just so many things that I don't know and this is driving me crazy. My plan is to just bide my time and go about my usual day to day business and pretend to be just a normal boy. Hopefully I'll find out why I've got these special powers and what I'm supposed to do with them.

My mum comes in to read to me at bed time. I love that time of day. I can relax. I don't have to think about Big Ears. I've got loads of books in my bedroom. I love reading. I've got loads of history books. History is my favourite subject. I've got loads of adventure books. And I've got loads of comics and I mean loads. I've probably got more than two hundred. I should count them all really. Maybe I will tomorrow.

You would like my bedroom. I've got loads of animals in it. I've got lots of Teddy Bears from when I was young,

I've got loads of dinosaurs and I've got two guerrillas. One's big and the other one is small. The big one has got a hand up in the air and the other has got a hand down low. When I walk into my room I give the big one a high-five and I give the small one a low-five.

My mum came in that night and asked me what book I wanted her to read to me. I told her that I wanted a surprise. When I ask for a surprise book my mum gets me to close my eyes. Then she chooses a few books off the bookshelf and I point my finger at a specific book.

The book that I point to is the book that she reads to me.

I love the book that I chose for tonight. The book is all about the amazon rainforest. I could do a 'talkabout' on the amazon rainforest the next time we do a show, tell or talkabout at school. Did you know that some of the rivers in the rainforest are over a thousand kilometres long? And did you know that the rainforest covers more than eight million square kilometres? And did you know that over fifty per cent of all of the plants and animals on earth can be found living in the rainforests? I love it when mum reads to me from the rainforest book. I love the pictures as well. It would be great to spend some time living in the rainforest. Maybe when I learn to control my wizard powers I will go and spend some time in the rainforest. I would love that. If you like frogs you would love the rainforest. There are thousands of different kinds of frogs in the rainforest. And if you like butterflies you would love the rainforest too because there are thousands of butterflies as well.

When my mum finished reading she turned out the light. But I never went to sleep. I did something that was much better than going to sleep.

A funny feeling came over me. It was just like the feeling I had on the beach when I started my first wizard adventure. This time my powers never took me into a pirate adventure. This time I found myself sitting on a branch on a huge tree. I was probably about twenty metres from the ground and I was hanging on for dear life. I thought that I was in a rainforest. The trees and the leaves and the plants that were all around me were massive. They were maybe about a hundred times bigger than normal trees and plants. I've never seen anything like it. Even the trees and the plants in the rainforest books were not as big as this.

I decided that I would have to concentrate really hard to try to find out why my wizard powers had sent me here. Maybe this way I could find out why I've been given these powers, and maybe then I'll be able to find out how I can use them when I want to use them.

The tree that I was on was maybe forty metres high altogether, or at least that's how it felt. I decided to climb to the top so that I could have a good old look around. It was going to take me a long time, but it was worth it because I needed to find out every last thing that I could. The leaves were wet and glossy and it was a very long way down. Each time that I looked down I got very dizzy indeed – I did my best to keep looking up. Some of the animal sounds that I could hear were very loud and very frightening. They made me jolt so much, that every time I heard one of the huge animal roars or squawks I nearly lost my grip. There were some massive, and I mean really massive, fern like plants below me. However, I'm not sure that even they would be enough to protect me if I were to fall from such a height.

I certainly didn't want to find out by falling from such a great height.

I kept climbing further and further up the tree until I got onto one of highest branches, and I was high enough to see over all of the other trees around me. It was then that I discovered where I really was: I wasn't in the rainforest at all. This was much more exciting than the rainforest. The sight that I could see was perhaps the most exciting sight that anyone had ever seen. Standing in a big circle of maybe about twenty or more was a whole group of dinosaurs. I was so shocked I nearly lost my grip and fell the

45

forty metres or so to the earth below. It was the most fantastic sight that you could imagine. It was a massive group of triceratops. My powers had taken me two hundred million years back in time. I was in the Jurassic period. I was looking at dinosaurs. These were real dinosaurs and I was looking at them. I had never dreamt of anything so beautiful, so magnificent and so fantastic in all of my life. Wowee! What a sight!

"This is out of this world," I said.

There standing in front of me was a whole group of triceratops circled together. And I was clinging onto a giant tree and holding on for dear life. They were all moving around really slowly. Sometimes they dipped their necks and sometimes they lifted their necks up to have a good look all around. This was amazing. Then I noticed something even more amazing. There were several young triceratopses in the middle of the circle. It was as though all of the adult triceratops had gathered around the young ones to protect them. Maybe they were sensing danger. I knew I was.

Then I heard the biggest screeching sound that I had heard in my life. It was so loud and so powerful that the shock caused me to lose my grip and fall from the tree, but I didn't fall far. Within a second of falling I fell onto the wing of a flying dinosaur and I held onto his wing as tightly as I possibly could. This was utterly utterly fantastic. Not only had my wizard powers taken me back two hundred million years in time. But now I was hanging onto the wing of a pterodactyl and flying above a herd of triceratops. Wow! This was the most exciting adventure of a thousand lifetimes!

The pterodactyl that I was flying on came to a standstill on a treetop. He didn't seem to mind me hanging

onto his wing. I don't even think that he knew that I was there. Then I saw a really beautiful sight. I saw a little saltoplus wondering around by himself. He was so cute. He was only about sixty centimetres long. Oh, he was so cute! He looked as though he only weighed about two kilograms.

Then I saw a stegosaurus walk by. I was really worried for the little saltoplus. I thought the stegosaurus was going to eat him. The poor little thing was just wondering around without a care in the world. He didn't seem to realize that there was a huge stegosaurus lurking behind him. I wandered if that was why my wizard powers had brought me here. Maybe I was supposed to help the little saltoplus. Then I noticed that it didn't seem that he needed my help. The stegosaurus seemed perfectly happy eating plants. I wondered if that was all they ever ate; so the little saltoplus knew that he wasn't in any danger.

The pterodactyl took off again and I was once more flying around in the air, looking down at a whole load of the most fabulous dinosaurs in history. I saw a brachiosaurus eating stones. I couldn't believe what I was seeing, "why on earth was a brachiosaurus swallowing stones?" I thought. Then I realized that it was to help him digest his food. This confused me even more. How could I possibly know that? My wizard powers make me know stuff that I couldn't possibly know without my special powers. But what I didn't understand is why?

Not far from the brachiosaurus I saw a maiosaurus dig a big hole. She laid about twenty eggs in it. I was quite high up circling about in the sky, so it wasn't easy for me to see but I would say that each egg was about fifteen centimetres long.

A herd of dinosaurs were running along at quite some speed. My pterodactyl turned away from them so I couldn't get a close up look. I think that they were a herd of Apatosaurus. Then I flew over something that was very frightening indeed. I saw two huge dinosaurs head butting each other. They were pachysepholosaurus and they were engaged in a really massive fight. They bent their heads down low and ran straight into each other at top speed.

I thought that watching pachysepholosaurus fighting would be the most violent thing that I would ever see in my life. That was until I saw a tyrannosaurus rex pounce on another dinosaur. I couldn't even make out what kind of dinosaur it was. That's how furious the attack was, it was horrible. It made me feel sick. I had to look away.

My pterodactyl came to a standstill and I saw something that I could have happily of gone without seeing at any time in my life – ever! I saw a stegosaurus do a poo! Oh man! That is something that nobody should ever have to see or smell! Ugghh! It was absolutely disgusting. There has never been anything more horrible in the world, that you could ever imagine, that is anywhere near as horrible as a massive pile of stegosaurus poo. Ahhh! It was absolutely vile and he did about twenty five buckets full all in one go. My pterodactyl flew over it and I caught the whole horrible pong right up my nose. It nearly made me faint. I thought I was going to pass out. It made me feel all dizzy. I squeezed my eyes tight shut and when I opened them my mum was standing over me telling me it was time for school. She told me to go and have a shower and to get myself cleaned up for school. I left her in the bedroom stripping the sheets off my bed. I couldn't help smiling to myself. She thought that I had been sleeping all night. If only she knew where I had really been.

Chapter 4 - Finding Treasure

When I got to school that day my teacher was even more lovey dovey than usual. The first thing that she did when she saw me was to kneel down and do my shoelace up for me. Then she gave me one of her hugs, she does give lovely hugs. She told me that she hoped I had a lovely day. "Let's all have a lovely day", is her most favourite saying.

After registration she asked us if any of us had anything to show, tell or talkabout. I put my hand up to do a "talkabout," but I had decided not to talk about dinosaurs just in case

I let it slip out that I had actually seen dinosaurs. I don't know what my wizard powers are for, but I know that people would never believe me and they would probably laugh at me. I did do a talkabout the rainforest though. I told the class that some of the rivers in the rainforests are over three thousand kilometers long. I told them that the Amazon rainforest covers an area of 800 square kilometres. Then I told them that there were thousands of frogs and butterflies there and that over half of all the world's plants and animals could be found there. Mrs Smith said it was one of the best talkabouts that she had ever heard. She put a marble in the jar and she gave me a gold sticker to wear. I was really happy even though I knew that I would be in for a hard time from Big Ears. He always picks on people who do well in class. I hate him. I went to the sick and lazy room at dinner time to stay out of his way. If you go and say that you're not feeling well you don't have to go outside.

When everybody else was playing outside at dinner time my wizard powers took me on another adventure. I found myself in an old shack in the Caribbean. I was back with my pirate friends but this time we were in another part of the world. I was staring at some sand on the floor that had been covered in blood. The old pirate with the gold teeth who had started the tattoo on my last adventure was busy finishing it off. Every now and then he stopped to spit on the floor. He was chewing tobacco that made his gold teeth look black. There were other pirates sitting around the shack. They were taking refuge from the warm mid-day sun. Some were drinking rum and some were chewing on limes, but they were all talking about one thing. Billy the Blackheart was putting together a group of pirates that were going to steal back a treasure chest that had been stolen from him. He knew who had the treasure and he had a map that was going to lead him to it.

But to be one of the pirates that went on the mission you had to complete three tasks of bravery. The first task was to balance on a rope bridge which was two hundred feet above the sea. The next task was to spend ten minutes in a darkened shack with poisonous snakes, and the final task was to complete a three minute handkerchief fight with Michael the Muscle.

There was only one way that I was going to find out why I had been given these wizard powers and that was to throw myself into every possible experience when my powers took me on an adventure, and that's exactly what I did. The challenges were due to start at six o'clock and I told Blackheart that I wanted to be a part of them. We set off up and over some steep and dangerous rocks to the top of a hill overlooking the coast. There were two ropes crossing over the sea to a cliff maybe two hundred feet away. The task was to walk across on the lower rope whilst holding onto the rope above. The rocks and the sea were such a long way down that one slip would be

a fall to a certain death. Pirates are good at climbing up ropes and we're good at using rope bridges. One by one I saw pirates take to the task and complete it. When it came to my turn I inched my way onto the rope. I kicked a stone off the edge of the cliff and it took an awfully long time to bounce off the rocks and eventually fall into the sea below. I grabbed onto the rope tightly with both hands. I could hear my own heart thumping in my chest. I could hear every breath I took and I could feel every bead of sweat dripping from my face.

My wizard powers allowed me to know things like 'how to use a rope bridge'. I don't know how I knew, I just did. I used my knowledge to good effect. I summoned up every ounce of courage that I had and I focused upon every step that I had to take. In no time at all I was stepping off the other end of the rope feeling both triumphant and proud. That was one task down and I had two more to go.

Blackheart led us down the rock and over some sand dunes until we came up to an old deserted shack. There were about fifteen of us who successfully completed the first task. He told us that we would all have to go into the shack together and stand in there for a full ten minutes.

He had filled the shack with poisonous snakes. He warned us that it was going to be completely dark in there and that we would not be able to talk to each other or strike a match. If any of us were to leave the shack before the ten minutes were up we would fail the task and would not be allowed to join the mission.

Blackheart said that he had fed the snakes with mice and birds, so none of us should be bitten by them so long as the snakes weren't startled. All we had to do was keep calm and we would be fine. One by one, we filed into the hut leaving the brightness of the summer sun outside and entering a place of complete darkness. We all stood there in silence. Each was as brave as or braver than the man before him. I could hear teeth chattering and knees knocking but nobody made a move for the door. Not one single man tried to leave. After ten whole minutes we were let out to safety. It was a sweet feeling to discover that we had put our lives on the line for ten minutes and survived.

The final task was the handkerchief fight. We waited until nightfall and a big fire was lit on the beach. A three minute handkerchief fight with Mick the Muscle was by far the scariest of the three challenges. Mick was massive. He was about 6ft 10 inches tall. His muscles were like massive balls of steel. There's a famous story that pirates tell about Mick the Muscle. He was standing on the deck of a ship during a big sea battle. He was hit in the chest by a cannonball. The ball bounced off him and fell onto the deck. Mick then picked the cannonball up and threw it back across the water. So now you can see why a three minute handkerchief fight with Mick the Muscle is so frightening.

We all drew lots to see who would fight him first. I drew the first lot and it was me who was going to fight Mick first. All of the pirates sat by the side of the beach fire and I went over the hill with Billy the Blackheart to face Mick the Muscle. If I walked back the other pirates would know that I had lasted three minutes with Mick the Muscle. If I came back on a stretcher they would know that I hadn't! I came down the other side of the sand dune to where Mick the Muscle was waiting for me with his handkerchief in his hands. The area was lit by the bright stars and by an even brighter moon. I circled towards Mick and took a hold of his handkerchief. Just as I did that Billy the Blackheart called for us to stop there. He asked me if I thought that I could win a fight with Mick the Muscle and I told him that I knew I couldn't. Mick the Muscle roared with laughter and slapped me on my back. He hit with such force that I fell to the ground. That made Mick the Muscle and Billy the Blackheart laugh even louder. They told me that I had proved myself to be a brave pirate by taking the handkerchief. They told me that I was definitely coming on the raid. After three minutes I went back to join the other pirates by the camp-fire. When I got back to the top of the hill it was clear I was standing on my own two feet so all of the pirates cheered.

Out of the fifteen of us who started out on the trials, seven of us were chosen to go on the expedition. The others weren't quite brave enough. They were told to wait by the fire and keep it burning bright until we returned.

Billy the Blackheart, Joyless Jack and Mick the Muscle led us off in search of Billy's treasure chest. He knew who had it, he knew where it was and he had a plan to retrieve it. We set off in rowing boats inland towards an old shack where Billy knew the treasure was being kept. We rowed up the river for several miles and we stopped to pull some coconuts from a tree. We collected several sacks of coconuts and carried them on our way towards the shack. The men who had stolen the treasure were army rebels. They had men or guards stationed outside of the shack and more men inside. The two men standing outside were in for a nasty shock. Mick the Muscle sneaked around to the back of the shack and climbed up onto the roof. He jumped down from the roof of the shack and landed on the guards, knocking them to the ground. When the guards from inside came rushing out to see what all of the noise was, we started throwing coconuts down upon them. They soon scarpered and they left all the lovely loot for us.

When we arrived back on the beach
the fire was burning brightly and we
were given a party fit for returning

heroes. We had plenty of grog and fresh food cooked on the fire. The fiddles and the squeeze box players struck up the music and we danced and sang until the sun came up.

That was the best pirate adventure ever!

Chapter 5 – Banged up by Billy

Back in the classroom we were given a nice surprise. There are twins in our class and they were having a birthday party. I've been to their house before. It's a great place for a birthday party. There are lots of rooms to play in and lots of little rooms to hide in when you're playing hide and seek. There's a big garden behind the shed with little outside buildings and they have bouncy castles. In the field at the bottom of the garden a farmer keeps horses. They come up to the fence at the bottom of the garden and you can stroke them. The twins are called Molly and Caitlin and sometimes their mum gives us apples and we feed them to the horses. I would love to have my own horse. When I find out how to use my wizard powers properly I'll ride my very own stallion. A white one and we'll run like the wind. That would be really brilliant. I'm not sure that it would be quite as good as flying around on the back of a pterodactyl, but I suppose that there are very few rides that can match that for excitement.

Mrs Smith had been invited to Molly and Caitlin's party. That was really good because she said that she would organize all of the games. Mrs Smith is really good at organizing games. I was really looking forward to it. The only bad thing about the party was that all of the children in the class had been invited. That meant Billy Big Ears was going to be there. I decided that I was going to do my best to stay away from him and to do my best to make sure that he didn't ruin my whole day.

The party was brilliant – all of the adults stayed in a back room and had a party of their own. They were looking at plastic containers or perfume or something (adults are weird). We had a clown who was really funny. He beeped a horn whenever he ran around the room. He had flowers that grew out of his coat pockets and they squirted water in your face whenever he came close to you. He had big orange hair, and he wore a bright yellow jacket and green and red trousers. He had a massive pair of purple boots. He was really funny.

We had great party food. There were cakes and biscuits and a massive big bowl of jelly babies. All of the adults were still smelling perfume and stuff in the other room, and Molly and Caitlin's big sister was looking after us. She let us eat whatever we wanted. It was brilliant. Billy Big Ears took a great big drink of cola and then let out a huge burp. I hate to say it, but it was really funny. Then Molly and Caitlin started burping. Then we all started burping. It was really funny.

Then we went out and played on the bouncy castle. It was brilliant. We loved it. This was the biggest and bounciest bouncy castle that I had ever seen in my life. Then Billy Big Ears came on and he bounced so high that he fell out and hurt himself. Ha ha! You shouldn't laugh when somebody hurts themselves I know, but somehow it seems all right when it's Billy Big Ears. Mrs Smith was the first adult on the scene. She loved Billy up and he was fine. Mrs Smith loves everybody. I'm not sure that she would love Billy if she knew what a bully he was.

Mrs Smith stayed out and organized the party games. We played sand sea shore. That's really good; you have to jump either side of a line and if you land on the wrong side when Mrs Smith shouts out "Sand" or "Sea" or "Shore", then you're out. We played statues and thumbs up and musical chairs. Mrs Smith is really good at organizing games. We played make a snake, which is a game of tag. When you're tagged you have to link arms with all of the other children. It's great fun but I fell over. Mrs Smith was standing over me like a shot. She gave me one of her big hugs and loved me up. It didn't hurt much but

I did cut my knee a bit. Mrs Smith brought me in and put a bandage on my knee. She bent down to bite the end of the bandage and tape it up and when she stood up I said, "Is that blood on your lip?" She wiped her mouth quickly, saying, "Don't be silly". Then she sent me out to play.

We started to play hide and seek. That is the best game to play at Molly and Caitlin's house because there are so many places to hide. I hid in an old outside building that used to be used as a toilet years ago. It was a small brick building with a big heavy wooden door. You could just see some light coming through from under the door but apart from that it was completely dark. I stood in the dark hiding place for ages. I could hear people sneaking around outside and every now and then I could hear screams and laughter when somebody got caught. At one point somebody came close to where I was hiding. I could hear them moving about outside of the door. I held my breath so that they wouldn't know that I was inside. They moved away without finding me and I stayed as still as I could for ages. The noises outside grew quieter and quieter. I was loving it. I thought that I could end up winning the game. In the end

I couldn't hear any sounds at all from outside. I'd been in there for so long I began to wonder if the game had finished and they had all gone home and forgotten me. I stayed there for a bit longer because I didn't want to give up and find that they were still looking for me. In the end I decided that I was going to give up anyway because I couldn't stay in the dark any longer. I went to open the door but it wouldn't open. It was jammed shut and locked from the outside. I tried it again but I couldn't make it budge. It was stuck fast. I started screaming for help but nobody answered. They must have all gone home and forgotten me. I screamed and screamed but nobody came. I started to think of Billy Big Ears. I bet that he had done this to me. I started to think of all the horrible things that I would do to him to get him back. I screamed and screamed at the top of my voice for someone to come and get me out. I thought of what I would do if I could control my wizard powers. I thought about flying over Billy Big Ears on the back of a Pterodactyl. I would pick him up and fly him back over two hundred million years and I would get the Pterodactyl to fly over some fresh stegosaurus poo. Do you remember that I told you that they do a great big mound of it about twenty five feet high? Well I would drop Big Ears into it head first. He would be screaming and shouting and trying to fight his way out and he would be covered from head to foot in stegosaurus poo.

Eventually Molly and Caitlin's mum came to let me out. Mrs Smith and my mum loved me up and I could see Billy Big Ears was staring at me from one of the windows. I knew it was him. One day I will get even with him. I hate him. I hate him. I hate him. I hate him. I hate him!

Chapter 6 – Super Heroes

It was a busy night in New York. Cab drivers were honking their horns. The neon lights were shining brightly and people of all shapes and sizes moved with purpose around the busy sidewalks. My senses guided me towards a small bar. Everybody else walked past it, but I was drawn towards the low lit sign above its door.

"HEROS' BAR"

As I approached it I caught sight of my reflection in a shop window. I was a masked super hero. My cape was purple and cream.

I didn't know why people weren't asking me why I was dressed like a super hero. I decided to find out. I stepped in front of a passing stranger and said, "Hey mister! How come you don't think it's strange that I'm dressed like a super hero?"

He just walked straight past me without answering. I thought that was really rude so I asked somebody else the same question. She just put her hand in the air and called for a cab. She acted as though I wasn't even there. Then it occurred to me: the reason that nobody was talking to me was because nobody knew I was there. They couldn't see me.

"Wow!" I thought to myself. "That must be my super hero power, I must be invisible."

That was the best news that I could have heard. If I could choose any super hero power it would be to be invisible. I walked into the super hero bar and straight away I knew why nobody was going in there. Nobody knew that it was there. Wherever I looked in the bar all I could see was superheroes. They came in all different shapes and sizes, and all different colours and capes.

I walked along the side of the bar and everybody said hello to me. Everybody knew me. They called me

'Dick'. The barman poured me a drink and called me 'Mac'. That confused me. I didn't know if my name was Dick or Mac. Then I realized something, the barman called everybody Mac. There was a very stretchy superhero at the far end of the bar. He stretched his neck up so that he could see me over the crowd. He stretched his arm out about fifteen metres to give me a high five. Then he pulled his head back down and drew his arm back in. He just carried on with his conversation as though it were the most ordinary thing in the world for somebody to be able to stretch like that.

So there I was saying hello to all of these fabulous superheroes, with all of their fabulous costumes, when all of a sudden a superhero appeared right in front of us. First there was a flash of smoke, and when the smoke cleared there was a super hero standing there dressed in a black cape with silver edges.

He was carrying a clipboard and he said, "OK. Hold up everybody. I won't keep you long. I just need to make a note of all of the good deeds that you have done this week and then I will leave you to it."

The stretchy superhero that I had just given a high-five put his hand up. Everybody laughed when his hand hit the ceiling, so he shrugged his shoulders and drew his hand into normal size. He said that he had rescued a family who were drowning in a river. He told us that their boat had capsized in a storm, so he stretched his arm out to pull them from the sea. He straightened the boat up then he put each of the family members back onto it and then pulled the boat into safety. Everybody clapped their hands and gave him a big round of applause. He seemed really popular. Everybody fell silent waiting for the next superhero to tell their story. Nobody was ordering drinks now. The barman kept himself busy by wiping glasses.

Some superheroes told of how they rescued people from cars. Others told how they rescued people from fires. One superhero told how she had rescued a kitten from a tree. She got a special round of applause. Then a massive super hero stood up. He must have been six foot ten inches. He had muscles everywhere. You could see his muscles bulging through his costume. He stood up and he got a round of applause just for standing up. He said that he had sorted out the dogs again. Everybody laughed. It turned out that "the Dogs" was the name given to superheroes who had gone bad. They used their superpowers to do evil. Muscleman didn't like it when a superhero turned bad. When he was asked what he did he just flexed his muscles and said, "The usual", and everybody laughed. The superhero in black made a note of it and muscleman sat back down.

A group of superheroes were sitting quietly in the corner. They raised their hands. They told us all about a very dangerous mission that they had carried out. There had been a bad disaster in Japan. It caused many people to lose their homes and it caused massive mudslides which swept many people away. The superheroes told of how they used all of their powers to rescue those being swept away. It sounded like a very long and very scary ordeal. When they finished telling their story everybody stood up and gave them a huge round of applause.

The superhero in black made some final notes on his clipboard. He said, "Well done everybody. Keep up the good work."

Then there was a flash and a puff of smoke and he was gone.

Everybody returned to doing what they were doing before he appeared.

I decided to move quickly. I didn't know how long my wizard powers would keep me here. I could find myself back at home, at school, on a bus, or anywhere and it could happen at any minute. I needed to get moving as quickly as I could to find out why my powers had brought me here and to find out what I was supposed to do with them.

I walked outside and straight away I enjoyed being invisible. I walked right in front of people and pulled faces at them, but they just looked straight through me as though I wasn't there. I decided to jump up and down and wave my hands around and that's when I had the shock of my life. I found that when I jumped I could just keep going up and up and up. In fact when I jumped, I could jump as high as a sky-scraper building. It was fantastic. I came back down to the ground then I bounced back up as high as I wanted to go. It was like being at the fairground on the best ride that had ever been invented.

I heard somebody mention the word 'power'. I wondered if they were talking about a super power so I listened more closely. It turned out to be a garage mechanic talking about a car engine. I looked around to see where he was and to my surprise I realized that he was nearly two hundred metres away. This was incredible. I had three super powers. I was invisible. I could jump as high as the tallest building in New York and I could listen in on conversations from nearly two hundred metres away. "Wowee!"

I could hear some interesting music high above me. It was coming from the twenty seventh floor of a skyscraper. So I just bounced up there to see what was going on. There was a girl in her room. I'd guess that she was about twelve years old. She had a towel around

her body and another one on her head. She was singing with a 'karaoke' machine and she was dancing around her room. It was good fun watching her but I bounced back down to the ground. I didn't know why my wizard powers had brought me here and I didn't know why they had given me superpowers, but I was pretty sure that I was supposed to use them for something more than watching a girl sing and dance in her bedroom.

I heard an argument taking place a few blocks away, so I bounced down there to find out what was going on. There was a woman in a room shouting at her husband. He had come in late and she was giving him a good telling off. I didn't want to listen to any more of that, so I bounced back down to the ground.

I bounced around for a while, listening in on peoples' private conversations and looking at them in their apartments when they thought that they were alone. It was good fun but I felt that I should be doing something much more important with my powers. Then it occurred to me: I was probably meant to find stuff out. I had the perfect power to be a private detective. Then I remembered what the other superheroes were calling me: 'Dick'. That must be it. Maybe I'm 'SuperDick'. A private Dick is what the Americans call a private detective. So if that's what my wizard powers had brought me here for, I now had to find out what it was I was supposed to detect.

Oh, this was really frustrating! I had all of the powers that I needed to be the greatest private detective that the world had ever known, but I had no way of finding out what I was supposed to detect.

I didn't know how much time I had, but I knew that my experiences up until now showed me that my wizard powers were not going to keep me here for very long. I needed to make myself busy and try and gain as much knowledge as I could. I decided to go to the very top of American cultural life. I made super bounces all across America until I came to the Whitehouse. I bounced right along to the door of the Whitehouse and walked right on in without anybody stopping me. I went along to the President's Oval office and sat in the President's seat. Soon after I arrived the President arrived with his senior staff. I stood by the side of the desk as they took their seats. They talked about their troops in the army. They talked about a visit from the Chinese Premier. They talked about climate change and they talked about taxes. Wow! I was a wizard with the most amazing superpowers and I had the most boring hour of my entire life. I thought that listening to the President of the United States

of America would be fun, but it was boring, boring, boring. The last thing that I remember was falling asleep.

Chapter 7 – Nice Vampires

Mum poured a big bowl of cereal for me. They were so cool. They had chocolate in them and they turned the milk a chocolate colour. When I was walking to school I could hardly keep my eyes open. I was excited about my wizard powers making me a superhero, but I was disappointed that I wasted so much time listening to the President of the United States of America bang on about the boring stuff for an hour. During show, tell and talkabout I told everybody that there's a secret bar in New York where superheroes meet. I told them that a superhero dressed all in black with silver lines on his cloak stops by each week to make a note of all of the good deeds that they do. Mrs Smith gave me one of her lovely hugs and told me that I had a wonderful imagination. Then I told her that superheroes who go bad are called 'dogs', and that a superhero called 'Muscleman' sorts them out. Then I told them that the Chinese Prime Minster was going to announce plans for a visit to America, and that the President of America was going to announce tax increases. It was fun telling people these things. But when it was announced on the news that the Prime Minister of China was planning a visit to America and it was announced that the American President was going to put taxes up, I had to pretend that they were just lucky guesses. I decided that I should be more careful in the future about telling information that I could only know because of my wizard powers. I really want other people to know that I'm a real boy wizard, but I think it's best that I keep it to myself until the time is right. I don't know when that will be.

I didn't know when my next wizard adventure would be, but I was surprised to find out that it was going to be on that very day. I was yawning my way through the day. I was always tired when I came back from one of my wizard adventures, but today I felt more tired than usual. It was as though all of the bouncing across America had worn me out.

We had a nice easy lesson to start the day. It was shared reading. Today I was going to read to a young girl from a lower class. I read to her first and then she reads to me. It's really good. It's one of my favourite lessons.

Whilst I was listening to her read to me my next adventure began. It was only a few hours since my wizard powers took me to the United States of America. This time they took me to a place that couldn't have been more different. I wasn't a superhero this time. I was a local newspaper reporter at a village fete. I was walking around making notes for an article for the local newspaper all about the fete. I was given lots of jam and scones to taste. All of the jams and all of the scones were homemade, and there was a competition to find out who could make the best. There were jams made out of blueberries, and blackberries, and strawberries, and all kinds of other berries. I loved it. I think the jam tasting at the village fete was the best thing that I had done on any wizard adventures. All of the people were so nice. I don't know how they could manage to eat so many different jams. I met Mrs Boothroyd. She was the winner from last year. She could not have been lovelier. She sat me down, fed me lots of little jam scones and dolloped a spoonful of fresh double cream on each one. Mrs Higgingbottom was really nice as well, she offered to show me around. She brought me to the 'Tombola' and the 'Shove a penny'. She brought me to see the

Vicar and the Vicar's wife. They had big smiling faces. In fact everybody had a big smiling face. I had never seen so many big smiling faces in all my life. There's no place nicer than a beautiful English village on a beautiful summer's day.

The question I asked myself was, "Why would a happy smiling place like this need a real boy wizard?" I liked being there. Well, I loved being there. I couldn't think of a nicer place to be. I just couldn't think why my wizard powers would bring me there. It was just a nice place, full of nice people. I made up my mind: the newspaper article that

I would write would be all about the nice news of the village and the fete, and the nice news of all the kindly smiling people there.

However, all of my wizard powers failed to stop me doing something very stupid indeed. I trod on a garden rake and the handle of the rake flew up and hit me in the face. I was seeing stars for a moment. Then each of the people that I had seen during the day started appearing in front of me. Each of them appeared as though they were drifting in on a cloud and that they were drifting away again. Their faces were now smiling wider than ever. Mrs Boothroyd, Mrs Higgingbottom, the Vicar and the Vicar's wife. They were all there. They all had red around their mouths. This had gone from being the nicest adventure that my wizard powers had taken me on, to the weirdest adventure.

The question that I kept asking myself was, "Why have all of these nice people got red around their mouths?" Then the answer occurred to me. They must be vampires. Not the kind of vampires that lie in the dark and kill people. No, these were the nice kind. The kind that bend down to talk to you or to cuddle you, but sneak a drop of blood out of your neck without you knowing. They don't kill you, they just make you feel a bit faint.

Among all of the visions of the people from the garden fete their appeared a new vision. It was Mrs Smith. She also had red all around her mouth. She must be a nice vampire as well. She was calling my name and gradually saying, "Come on".

She was saying, "Come on, you're all right now. You just felt a little faint."

I couldn't believe it. My own teacher was a vampire. She had something in common with all of the people from the fete – she was very very nice. That must be how they disguise themselves. If you know somebody who is really really nice. The kind of person who wants to give you hugs and look after you; just be a bit careful. They might be nice vampires who want to suck a bit of your blood from you. Don't worry, nice vampires won't kill you but they might make you feel a bit faint.

"How are you feeling?" Mrs Smith said.

"I'm much better thank you", I said gently, pulling my neck away from her.

"You're looking a bit brighter. I think you felt a little faint."

I think she was right and I think I know why. Mrs Smith told me to take the little girl down to the Head Teacher to get a smiley face sticker for being such a good reader. I like going to see the Head Teacher. He gives you lots of stickers for doing good work. He's really nice. As the

Head Teacher bent down to put the sticker on the little girl, it occurred to me that he might be a vampire too. I pulled the sticker off him and put it on the little girl myself. I led her away saying, "Thank you very much sir!"

Let that be a warning to you. If you have a really nice teacher or Head Teacher, just be a bit wary. They might turn out to be nice vampires!

Chapter 8 – Becoming a Wrestler

At show, tell or talkabout the next day, one of the girls in our class talked about her holiday. It did sound very good although it really couldn't compare to one of my wizard adventures. The girl had been to Disneyworld. She even met Mickey and Minnie Mouse, and had her picture taken with them. The rides that she went on sounded fabulous and the food sounded wonderful. It seemed as though she had syrup and cakes with everything. The best of her treats were saved until last. On the plane ride home one of the stewardesses spilled some coffee on her lap, and for a treat they brought her up to see the captain. Can you imagine actually sitting next to the captain in the cockpit whilst he is flying the plane? That sounds like a really fantastic thing to do. Even I thought that would be a fantastic adventure, and it's hard to impress the real boy wizard. I wanted to tell the class about some of my wizard adventures but I somehow knew that I mustn't.

Today was a big day for our class. We were going to an outward bound centre. It's really good fun there. I've been there before. You can go on a climbing frame and you can do abseiling. I love the abseiling, that's my favourite part of the whole day. I did it head first once. It was fantastic. You can do air rifle shooting and archery, and in the afternoon you can go on an indoor ski-slope. That's really good fun as well.

I wanted to sit at the back of the coach but 'you know who' was sat there. I decided to sit up at the front by Mrs Smith so that I could avoid him. I thought that going to the outward bound centre would be the most exciting thing that happened to me that day but I was wrong. No sooner had I sat down on the coach than my wizard powers took me on a new adventure.

I found myself in America again. I couldn't believe the size of my legs. I was looking down at the biggest muscular legs I had ever seen in my life. And I wasn't alone. I was sat in a dressing room with about a dozen of the biggest most muscular men you have ever seen in your life. I was a wrestler. Wow! I couldn't believe it. I love wrestling, and here I was a real wrestler with all of these other wrestlers. I wished that I could use my wizard powers to magic me back to the school bus. I'd grab Billy Big

Ears off the back seat, throw him down the bus and he could sit next to Mrs Smith.

I did what all of the other wrestlers did. I stretched all of my muscles and I lifted some weights to get the blood pumping around my body.

One of the wrestlers was wearing exactly the same costume as I was. He started pushing his shoulder into me and I knew that I had to do the same back to him. I couldn't believe how strong I was. The muscles in my arms were as hard as huge balls of steel.

The next thing that happened to me was the most exciting thing that happened to me in all of my wizard adventures. I stood by the entrance waiting to be called into the arena. The music was loud and raucous; and the vast crowd was cheering, whistling and chanting.

A huge roar went up around the Arena and the spotlights shone on my opponent. He was massive. He was a man mountain. I've never seen muscles like his before in my whole life. My muscles were big. His muscles were outrageous. He walked down to the ring and climbed into it. He took off his maroon cape and whirled it around his head and hurled it into the crowd.

That was the man that I was going to be wrestling with. I had butterflies flapping wildly in my stomach. The spotlights shone on me. It was my time to step forward. The sound of the crowd hit my ears with huge ferocity. I climbed into the ring, held my arms up high and gave a little bow to the four sides of the crowd.

The announcements were made and the bell rang. The referee stepped to one side and I faced my opponent man to man. Then the force of his power hit me like a freight train. He hit me with a bump and I fell, landing down on my back on the mat. I climbed back to my feet and shook my head in an effort to clear it. I gathered my senses and my courage and ran towards him again. This time he put his arm out straight and hit me with a clothesline that took me off my feet, once again I found myself flat on my back on the mat. I crawled back up to stand on my feet when suddenly I was hit by a dropkick. Both of my opponent's feet came flying through the air and hit me hard, knocking me flat on my back and back down to the mat. Then he fell on top of me and wrapped both of his legs around my neck. He wrestled my head and neck backwards and forwards; crashing it into the mat from left to right and from right to left, again and again.

I forced myself free and I ran towards the ropes. I bounced off them and I ran back towards him giving him a kick to his middle. When he bent down gasping for breath I bulldogged him by grabbing him around the head and forced his head into the mat. I climbed up onto

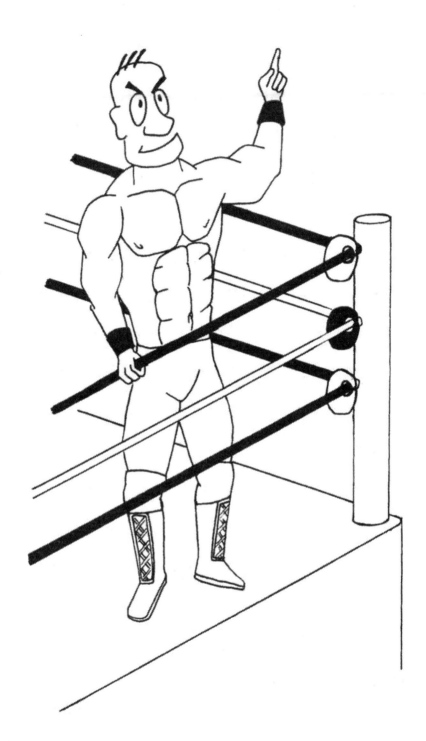

the turnbuckle and I jumped off it, driving my elbow into his chest. Now it was his turn to stagger around the ring desperately trying to suck air into his lungs.

The audience were chanting his name and he was far from ready to be finished off. He ran towards me again and shoulder charged into my stomach. He knocked all of the air out of me and I fell back to the mat.

I walked back into the corner and waved my hand in the air. He had hurt me badly. He hit his chest and roared to the crowd and the crowd roared back at him. I took the opportunity to attack him. I ran towards him and grabbed him with one hand over his shoulder and the other between his legs. I lifted him in the air and slammed his whole body onto the mat. I ran back to the ropes and bounced off them to charge towards him once again, but he jumped to his feet and grabbed me around the head. He held me in a headlock and ran me around the ring, forcing my head into the turnbuckle. I fell, flat on my back on the mat. I was seeing stars.

The referee was told to start counting. He thought he had me beat and I knew that I had to summon up all of my strength and get back to my feet. The referee got to seven and I jumped up. I lifted his arm above my head. I put his other arm around my waist. I lifted him up over my shoulder and dumped him down on the mat. I ran back to the ropes and bounced back off them, jumping in the air and landing flat down in a huge body splash on him.

I staggered back to the corner and lent on the turnbuckle. Within a second he ran towards me with a huge body avalanche and crashed into the turnbuckle. He ran towards me to do it again, but I quickly moved out of the way. He ran headfirst into the turnbuckle and knocked himself out.

I jumped down on him and sat on his chest. I locked his head in a tight leg lock. He screamed and hit the mat with his hands. I dragged him to his feet and jumped up. I slammed his whole body in a vertical press.

He forced me from him and ran back to the ropes. I got to my feet and he attacked me with a series of chops that left me dazed and confused. He followed up with more chops. First he hit me with a backhand chop, then a cross chop, and finally a forehand chop. He then chopped me on the neck with both hands. I was standing in the middle of the ring and he ran back to the ropes. He came at me with speed and agility, hitting me with a flying forearm smash.

I could only gather my senses as best I could and he ran towards me again. I could tell that we were both coming to the end of our energy reserves so I had to go for my finishing move. I caught a hold of his arm and put him into a fireman's lift. I brought him down to my knee and hurled him to the floor. I fell on top of him, I hooked both legs and the referee counted one, two, three! I had won and the crowd went wild. I wasn't expected to win and the crowd loved it. They took me to their hearts and cheered me wildly.

I was battered and dazed and sore and weary. I was carried from the ring on the shoulder of security guards. Everybody wanted to touch me and give me high-fives.

I think that the battering that I took really did knock the stuffing out of me. The following morning I had to walk very slowly to breakfast as I was aching. I sat down to breakfast and ate my cornflakes; very, very slowly.

My mum sounded really cross with me when she came downstairs. She said that she would have to spend half the day sewing up Keran, the giant gorilla in my bedroom. She said his stuffing was all coming out. My mum gets upset about the strangest things. I had far more important things to think about. I had been on yet another adventure and it was probably the best adventure that my wizard powers had taken me on. Yet after all of the great adventures I was no nearer to knowing why I had been given these real boy wizard powers, and I was no nearer to knowing what I was supposed to do with them.

Chapter 9 – What now?

Being a real boy wizard is the greatest adventure that any boy could have. I guess that it would be the same for a girl if there's a girl somewhere who has the same powers. There are female dinosaurs, there are female pirates, there are lots and lots of female wrestlers (and they are ferocious) and there are female vampires. It makes sense to suppose that there might be a girl or any number of girls, who have the same powers that I have. Maybe there are and maybe they know how to use their powers, and maybe they know what they are supposed to do with them. My life has become one long series of questions ever since I first discovered my wizard powers. Unfortunately I still don't have any answers.

I keep thinking that there must be a reason why my powers sent me to the places and the times that I have travelled to, but I haven't got a clue what those reasons are. Maybe somebody who has the same powers as me will read this book and get in touch with me. All I can do is go about my life and try to make sense of everything.

The day after my last adventure I went to school as usual. I like school and I like my teacher (just as long as she stays away from neck). The only person I don't like at school is Big Ears. I was going about my business in a normal way. I was a bit stiff after my wrestling adventure. Big Ears was being his normal self. I came across him at lunchtime. He had tied a girl up with a skipping rope. It was the nice little girl who reads to me in shared reading. My first thought was to run and find a dinner supervisor. I could see that the rope was really hurting the little girl so I went over to them. I pushed

Billy out of the way and I started to untie the rope from around the little girl. Billy ran back at me and charged into me. I picked him up in a fireman's lift and slammed him to the floor. Once I had untied the little girl, I told Billy that I wouldn't let him bully me or anybody else ever again.

When we got back into class we had a show, tell or talkabout. I put my hand up and asked Mrs Smith if I could talk about bullying. She said that I could, so I told her that there was a bully in our class and that he had bullied everybody. I told her that it wasn't fair, because every time we told an adult about him nothing was ever done about it. Mrs Smith asked all of the children if this was true and they all said it was. I never told her the name of the bully but she knew who it was. Even if she didn't already know, it was obvious that Billy was the bully because when we were talking everybody was looking at him.

Just at that moment the Head Teacher came into the class. The little girl that Billy had tied up was with him.

He said, "It has come to my attention that there is a boy in this class who used a rope to tie up this little girl at lunchtime."

Everybody looked at Billy again. This time he went really red. Mrs Smith told the Head Teacher that we were just discussing bullying. She said, "It seems as though there has been a bully in our midst for quite some time now."

The Head Teacher told Billy to go and wait outside his office. Then he told me that he had heard how brave I was, standing up to him and helping the little girl. He went to put one of his special Head Teachers gold stickers on me. I pulled back from him a little and took it from his fingers instead. I pulled my shirt up around my neck. I may not know why I have the powers of a real boy wizard but I know that I'm going to remember the things that I have learnt on my adventures.

Well, that's it. That's my story. If you've got the same powers as me, at least you know you're not alone.

Other titles by E.R.Reilly

Harriet the Horrible

Best Friend

Rashnu

Tall Tales

One Boy One Dream One Club

The Look Outs

The Children's Lottery

The Look Out's and the Stolen Puppies

Visit the website

www.er-reilly.co.uk